WES MAGEE
*The Ghost Train Ride
at Fangster's Fair*

WES MAGEE was born in Greenock, Scotland. He
worked as a bank clerk and National Serviceman
before studying at University of London where he
began writing. He was a teacher and then Head
Teacher at large Primary schools in Wiltshire,
Hertfordshire and Humberside until resigning to
become a full time author in 1989. He has published 6
poetry collections for adults, and over 100 books for
children. He regularly makes author visits to schools
and libraries nationwide, speaks at conferences, and
tutors at writing courses for adults.

Also by Wes Magee

WES MAGEE

The Ghost Train Ride at Fangster's Fair

CROMER

PUBLISHED BY SALT PUBLISHING

12 Norwich Road, Cromer, Norfolk NR27 0AX
United Kingdom

© Wes Magee, 2012

The right of Wes Magee to be identified as the
editor of this work has been asserted by him in accordance
with Section 77 of the Copyright, Designs and Patents Act 1988.

First published 2012

Printed in the UK by the MPG Books Group

Typeset in Oneleigh 11 / 14

ISBN 978 1 84471 331 8 paperback

1 3 5 7 9 8 6 4 2

for

Alexander, Benjamin, Charlotte,
Daniel, Janet, Jonathan, Kingsley,
Miranda, Natalie, and Rosylyn.

Simply, the best.

CONTENTS

'I hear the Ghost Train rumbling
along the track . . .'

—'(Waiting for) The Ghost Train'
MADNESS

The Ghost Train Ride
at Fangster's Fair

Miss it
if you dare!

FANGSTER'S FAIR
IS HERE!

At The Showground
all week

Monday thru Sunday
Come and have a Funday!

Terrific Thrills!
Daunting Dares!
Spectacular Spills!
Spooky Scares!

Emma uses her mobile phone
to call her friend, Josh.

EMMA:

"They say the Funfair's really great.
Josh, shall we go? Is it a date?"

JOSH:

"Sounds good, Emma. It should be rare.
Ten minutes . . . and I'll meet you there."

AT FANGSTER'S FAIR

Evening. The sun's gold disc has just gone down.
A crescent moon floats high above the town.

Crowds watch as bikers scorch the *Wall of Death*.
Fire-eating men *whoosh* flames of red-hot breath.

Shrill shrieks and squeals as *Rollercoasters* plunge.
    *"Clout Charlie Clown!
    Ten pence a sopping sponge!"*

Some *Ride-A-Log* where waters foam and swirl.
Rap music echoes as the *Waltzers* whirl.

The painted *Dodgems* whine and spark and crash.
    *"Shoot down the ducks,
    and win yourself hard cash!"*

The *Fortune Teller* strokes her one-eyed cat.
Tall mirrors make Em thin . . . make Josh look fat.

Evening. Stars shine. A chill invades the air.
    *"Come on, you two,
    and give yourselves a scare.
    Come on, and ride the Ghost Train
    . . . if you dare!"*

EMMA:

"Let's ride the Ghost Train, Josh. Okay?
I've got spare cash. My treat. I'll pay."

JOSH:

"*You'll* pay. I like it, Em. You're on!
But, *ghosts*? I bet we won't see one!"

THROUGH THE COBWEBBED CURTAIN

Two tickets bought, they climb aboard
into an open car.
There, side by side, they sit and wait,
and grip a cold steel bar.

A minute . . . then with a whiplash jolt
the rattling Ghost Train starts.
Their eyes grow wide as up ahead
a cobwebbed curtain parts.

Into the darkness rolls the train
on narrow, rusty rails,
and in the fusty, musty gloom
they hear weird cries and wails.

A graveyard smell, a frowsty scent
is hanging in the air.
Squat spiders dangling from the roof
trail long legs through their hair.

The Ghost Train ride is underway.
Will it be fake . . . or fright?
Now Em and Josh see up ahead
a light . . .

       . . . a glowing light.

EMMA:

"Josh, look! A glowing light ahead!
It's got the faintest tinge of red."

JOSH:

"Just listen to those ghastly groans
. . . and I can see white *b-b-bones*!"

(The Ghost Train stops beside a gloomy cavern . . .)

THE CAVERN BY THE TRACK

The Ghost Train
shudders to a stop
where the reddish light
is glowing.

There in a cavern
by the track
five skeletons
are showing
white bones,
white bones,
white bones . . .

THE SKELETONS' SONG

"Ohhhhhhhhhh,
we are five swaying skellies
and we quake and shake like jellies.
Yes, we're nifty boneline dancers,
and such itchy twitchy prancers.
Our hot rhythm's finger-snapping
when we set toe bones a-tapping,
and with arms bones interlocking
our old knobbly knees start knocking
 when the Ghost Train makes a stop,
 when the Ghost Train makes a stop.
 Wooooooooooooooo!"

 "Ohhhhhhhhhh,
 clip and clap
 and snip and snap
 just watch us make
 our elbows flap
 and hear our toes
 go tap tap tap
  when the Ghost Train makes a stop,
  when the Ghost Train makes a stop."

"Ohhhhhhhhh,
we're entertaining skellies,
minus eyeballs, brains and bellies.
We will make you smile and giggle
as we jump and jive and jiggle,
but remember we're *real* bonies
not your painted plastic phonies.
So, believe it kids, we're scary
and you're right to be bewary
  when the Ghost Train makes a stop,
  when the Ghost Train makes a stop.
      Wooooooooooooooooooooooo!"

"Ohhhhhhhhh!
clip and clap
and snip and snap
just watch us make
our elbows flap
and hear our toes
go tap tap tap
  when the Ghost Train makes a stop,
  when the Ghost Train makes a stop.
      Yeah!"

(The Ghost Train starts up and rattles along the
twisting, turning track . . .)

8

SKELETONS IN THE MIND

And as
the Ghost Train
rattles on
it leaves
the skeletons
behind,
but pictures
of those
bony bods
stay
printed
in
the
mind,
stay
printed
in
the
mind

.

.

.

.

.

.

.

THE NEXT STOP

The Ghost Train
judders round a bend,
then stops
above a pit.

Em and Josh
lean from their car
and stare
down

i
n
t
o

i
t
.
.
.
.
.
.
.

EMMA:

"Wow, Josh! What flames! What searing heat!
It's toasting my poor toes and feet!"

JOSH:

"Down there it's like a fiery well.
I think we're looking . . . into *Hell!*"

(Emma and Josh feel hotter . . . and hotter . . .)

THE PIT OF FIRE

They see hot, raging fire
　　with flames licking higher.
　　　　Incandescent pink smoke
　　　　　　makes them splutter and choke.

There's a real scorching heat
　　that is roasting their feet.
　　　　Trunks of oak and ash flare
　　　　　　in the furnace down there.

As the inferno sears
　　it is grilling their ears.
　　　　The fire is *so* bright,
　　　　　　but . . . *who's* frying tonight?

Now they hear from the flames
　　voices calling their names.
　　　　From the fire's roar and din . . .

　　　　　　　　"*Em and Josh,*
　　　　　　　　come on in . . ."

　　　　　　　　　　"*Em and Josh*
　　　　　　　　　　come on in . . ."

(Just in time, the Ghost Train rattles on . . .)

ONCE MORE . . .

Once more
  the Ghost Train
    rattles on,
      and leaves
        the Pit of Fire
        behind,
        but voices
      calling from
    the flames
      still
        echo
          in
              the
                mind,
              still
            echo
          in
          the
          mind
            .
              .
                .
                  .
                    .
                  .
                    .

EMMA:

"Where are we *now*? *Phew*, what a smell!
It's making me feel quite unwell."

JOSH:

"The pong's from that old bubbling pot.
I think we've reached . . . a Witches' Grot!"

*(The Ghost Train screeches to a halt
beside a smelly, squalid cave . . .)*

AT SIX WITCHES' GROT

It's grim and it's gloomy,
and the whole place is slimy.
Cobwebs hang from the walls
and the floor's greasy-grimy.

A three-legged cauldron
with a vile stew that's bubbly.
'*Ye Spellz*' book on a hook,
and six witches . . . all stubbly.

Cockroaches and earwigs,
and a plague of green grundies.
Hey, see there, hung to dry,
the six witches', er, *undies*.

The Ghost Train has stopped
at the Six Witches' coven.
There's a *terrible* smell
and . . . what's *that* in the oven?

(Emma and Josh gaze amazed
as the six witches dance around the cauldron
and prepare a spell . . .)

THE WITCHES' BREW

The warty witches cast their spell.
They flick in scabs, head-lice as well,
    then skip around the pot.
The tatty-haired ones chuck in fleas,
a pig's intestines, rancid cheese,
    and plums that stink of rot.

They hurl in headaches, books by Dahl,
a rusty key, a grizzly's snarl,
    then stir with baseball bats.
Watching this spree from fungal logs
are burping toads and belching frogs
    and *thirteen* hissing cats.

The stubbly-chinned ones boil the brew.
They are one itchy-witchy crew
    as they perform and dance.
They cancan round the pot like goats.
They show ripped knickers, petticoats,
    while cackling, *"Vive La France!"*

Then in a purple cloud of smoke
the toothless uglies give a croak
    and vanish from the Grot!
What's left behind? One crumpled hat,
a well-scuffed boot, a crying cat,
    and vile stew in the pot.

The smell is turning Emma green,
while writhing shadows at the scene
    send shivers down her back.
A whistle blows. The Ghost Train starts
and with a whiplash jolt departs
    and rumbles down the track . . .

THE GHOST TRAIN'S SONG

(as it rumbles along . . .)

Snickerty snee
    snickerty snack
        snickerty snackerty
          snickerty snack.
    Clickerty clee
  clickerty clack
  clickerty clackerty
over the track.
  Pickerty pee
    pickerty pack
        pickerty packerty
         pickerty pack.
    Flickerty flee
  flickerty flack
all the way there
and all the way back,
  all the way there
    and all the way back
  with a
flickerty
  flackerty
    flickerty
      flack!

THE TUNNEL WALL

The Ghost Train suddenly slows to a crawl.
Em and Josh see screens on the tunnel wall.

Videos are playing and music pounds.
Josh and Em tap feet to the funky sounds.

Screen after screen after screen is aglow
as Em and Josh view a freak 'Fashion Show'.

(TV screens line the tunnel walls,
and Emma and Josh are treated to some really freaky
    fashions . . . from Z–to–A . .)

THE FREAK FASHION SHOW

Emma and Josh see . . .

Zombies in Zinc Zoot-suits,
Yaks in Yellow Y-fronts,
Xposers in Xanthic X-ray specs,
Werewolves in White Wellingtons,
     and
Vampires in Violet Vests.

They see . . .
Uncles in Umber Underpants,
Trolls in Tangerine Tank-tops,
Skeletons in Snow-white Shawls,
Robots in Red Rubber,
     and
Quaggas in Quince Quilts.

They see . . .
Phantoms in Pink Pants,
Ogres in Orange Odd-socks,
Nasties in Nifty Necklaces,
Monsters in Mustard Mini-skirts,
     and
Loonies in Lemon Leotards.

They see . . .
Kangaroos in Khaki Knickers,
Jabberwockies in Jasmine Jeans,
Imps in Inky Inflatables,
Hags in Harlequin High-heels,
   and
Ghosts in Grey Gowns.

   They see . . .
Fiends in Flame Flip-flops,
Elves in Emerald Earmuffs,
Draculas in Disgustingly Dirty Denims,
Creepies in Crimson Cardigans,
   and
Banshees in Barely-there, Blue Bikinis.

   And . . . finally
Apparitions
   in
      Amber
         Antarctic
            Anoraks!

EMMA:

"Josh, *brrrr,* it's cold. There's such a chill.
I'm shivering. Hope I'm not ill."

JOSH:

"It *is* cold, Em. Why? I don't know.
But what's this now? Look, flakes of snow!"

(And as the Ghost Train rattles on,
the temperature suddenly drops.
Is it cold?
Hey, it really is!
Emma begins to shiver . . .)

THE NORTH WIND

The Ghost Train picks up speed, and then
      it rounds a bend
            and slows again.

A North Wind now sweeps down the track.
      There's Arctic snow
            upon its back.

The bitter wind makes Em desire
      a scalding drink
            and roaring fire,

but all she gets is frost-nipped nose
      and ice-pinched ears
            and frozen toes.

THE GRAVEYARD IN THE SNOW

The Ghost Train screeches to a stop.
Josh says, *"Let's take a break!"*
They step down from the open car
      and give cramped legs a shake.

They're in a graveyard, cold and bleak.
Snow lies on toppled 'stones.
Pale moonbeams light a ghostly scene
      of scattered skulls and bones.

The winter graveyard's freezing cold
but the starlit sky is clear.
As Em and Josh crunch through the snow
      what do they *see* . . .
               and *hear*?

(So, what do they see . . . and hear . . . ?)

SEEN . . . AND HEARD . . . IN THE GRAVEYARD IN THE SNOW

They *see* . . .
>> weathered tombstones like rotting teeth,
>> fading flowers and a withered wreath,
> the silent flight of a long-eared owl,
> a muddied spade and a broken trowel,
>> holly bushes with spikes and spears,
>> granite statues with their frozen tears.
> They *see* all these where chill winds blow
>>>> in the
>>>>> graveyard
>>>> in the
>>>>> snow.

They *hear* . . .
>> a coffin creak, a ghostly call,
>> rocks tumbling from the dry-stone wall,
> clock tolling in its crumbling tower,
> — twelve mournful strokes — the midnight hour,
>> dull thunder growling in the sky,
>> a groan of pain, a shout, a sigh.
> They *hear* all these where chill winds blow
>>>> in the
>>>>> graveyard
>>>> in the
>>>>> snow.

EMMA:

"That graveyard . . . creepy place, or what?
More scary than the Witches' Grot!"

JOSH:

"You've said it, Em. But what comes next?
This journey's got me *so* perplexed."

(It grows warmer as the Ghost Train rattles on . . .)

AND AS . . .

. . . the Ghost Train
            rattles on
                        it leaves
                                    the graveyard
                                        far behind,
                        but pictures
                    of that
                wintry place
                are frozen
                    in
                        the
                                mind,
                            are
                        frozen
                    in
                the
                mind
                    •
                    •
                        •
                            •
                                •
                            •
                        •
                            •

(A Railway Station comes in view.
    The Ghost Train approaches Platform Two . . .)

PLATFORM TWO

The Ghost Train
stutters up a slope.

A railway station
comes in view.

The engine stammers
to a stop

where hanging signs
read *'Platform Two'*.

EMMA:

"So many people. What a throng!
Josh, it's at least four hundred strong!"

JOSH:

"Not *people*. They're all *phantoms*, Em.
Ghosts . . . every single one of them!"

*(From the throng of phantom passengers
waiting on Platform Two
a song arises . . .*

THE PHANTOM PASSENGERS'
SONG

"Yes,
we are porter, stationmaster,
giggly girl with ghetto-blaster,
roller-skater hurtling faster,
fat man with left leg in plaster,
fleers from a flood disaster,
and one BBC broadcaster
    waiting here on Platform Two
    for our train long overdue."

"Yes,
we are Class 3C with teacher,
saintly nun and barefoot preacher,
barking dog (the noisy creature!),
student with his nose in Nietzsche,
tiny toddler who's a screecher,
and leggy blonde (a streaky bleacher)
    waiting here on Platform Two
    for our train long overdue.
        Now hear us cry
        boo boo
        boo
        boo!"

Information Note:
*(These phantoms
have been here,
you see,
since 5th of May in '63.
The station clock
stopped on that date,
hands fixed
in time
at 10 past 8 . . .)*

"Yes,
we are aunties Dot and Dora,
bearded underground explorer,
girl with ponytail (called Laura),
mooing cow — you can't ignore 'er,
antiques furniture restorer,
and a man asleep (the snorer!)
    waiting here on Platform Two
    for our train long overdue."

"Yes,
we are fireman, flautist, farmer,
handsome hunk who's quite a charmer,
Lulu and her laughing llama,
ladies who teach speech and drama,

nutters dressed in suits of armour,
and Big Bertha Betsy Barmer
     waiting here on Platform Two
     for our train long overdue.

       Now hear us cry
       boo boo
       boo
       boo!"

        Information Note:
        (These phantoms
        have been here,
        you see,
        since 5th of May in '63.
        The station clock
        stopped on that date,
        hands fixed
        in time
        at 10 past 8 . . .)

EMMA:

"Sorry, Phantoms, but we can't stay.
The Ghost Train's getting underway."

JOSH:

"You're dead right, Em. It's time to go.
'Bye, Phantoms. Hope *your* train will show."

THE GHOST TRAIN'S SECOND SONG

(as it continues to rumble along . . .)

Rickerty rack
  rickerty rong
    rickerty rackerty
      rickerty rong.
          Bickerty back
              bickerty bong
              bickerty backerty
          singing this song.
          Zickerty zack
              zickerty zong
                  zickerty zackerty
                  zickerty zong.
              Dickerty dack
              dickerty dong
          on up the track
        and rattling along
      on up the track
    and rattling along
      with a
          dickerty
              dackerty
                dickerty
                  dong.

EMMA:

"Josh, *things* are flying through the air.
I feel their fingers in my hair!"

JOSH:

"Look, scores of ghosts above the track!
Duck, Em, we're under spook attack!"

SPOOK ATTACK!

Above Em's head and Josh's hair
grey ghosts and spooks float in the air,
and in the tunnel's murk they cry
and try to grab the passers-by.
>*But, hey,*
>*the Ghost Train*
>*rattles on, on, on,*
>*the Ghost Train*
>*rattles on!*

Those bug-eyed spooks with razor-nails
scare Em and Josh with shrieks and wails.
Ghosts shaking rusty, clanking chains
are keen to dine on tasty brains.
>*But, hey,*
>*the Ghost Train*
>*rattles on, on, on,*
>*the Ghost Train*
>*rattles on!*

Sad spooks and ghosts up from the tomb
are floating in the tunnel's gloom.
Their fingers strain to clutch Em's coat
and reach to grab Josh by the throat.
> *But, hey,*
> *the Ghost Train*
> *rattles on, on, on,*
> *the Ghost Train*
> *rattles on!*

ROUND THE BEND

The Ghost Train speeds
        along the track
and leaves behind
        the spook attack.
        Are Em and Josh
    near journey's end?
                    Or
                    do
                more
                shocks
                    lie
                round
                    the
                    bend?

*(What's this?
A Crumbling Castle . . . ?)*

THE VAMPIRE

The Ghost Train stops with squeal of brakes.
Now Em and Josh see misty lakes,
and there perched high upon a hill,
a crumbling castle . . . silent, still.
From one ruined tower there comes a flight
of vampires in the moonlit night,
and as the seconds slowly drain
the red-eyed beasts head for the train.

> *(And what's that noise,*
> *that lonesome howl?*
> *A hungry werewolf*
> *. . . on the prowl?)*

As Em and Josh sit struck with fear
the sharp-toothed vampire bats draw near.
With lightning flash and thunder crack
one vampire lands beside the track
and changes to a man — *life-size!* —
with blood-tipped fangs and bloodshot eyes.
In cloak, top hat and silver cane
he stands before the steaming train.

(And what's that noise,
that lonesome howl?
A hungry werewolf
. . . on the prowl?)

The Vampire gives an evil leer
and orders Em and Josh, *"Come here!*
Come to my Castle, no delay.
I'll drink your blood 'til break of day!"
His raucous laughter floods the night
and fills shocked Em and Josh with fright,
but suddenly the Ghost Train starts
and with a whiplash jolt departs.

(Once more . . . that noise,
that lonesome howl.
A hungry werewolf
. . . on the prowl?)

EMMA:

"Josh, look ahead! A light! A light!
I think it means the end's in sight!"

JOSH:

"There's something here, Em, round the bend.
The cobwebbed curtain! It's the end!"

(The cobwebbed curtain!
Is the Ghost Train's journey at an end?
Well, almost . . .)

BACK THROUGH THE COBWEBBED CURTAIN

The cobwebbed curtain
    jerks apart.
        They're now back where
            they made a start.

        With hiss of steam
        and clang and pop
    the Ghost Train shudders
to a stop.

Em and Josh puff cheeks,
    climb out.
        "We made it . . . in one piece!"
            they shout.

        They do high fives
        and hug and cheer.
    Then Josh says,
"Let's get out of here!

*(Emma and Josh
are back at Fangster's Fair.
But something's . . . something's . . . not quite right . . .)*

IT'S LATE

As Em and Josh walk from the hissing train
they find themselves in chilling, drizzly rain.

High overhead the frosty stars look down.
The crescent moon floats high above the town.

Josh looks around, and says, *"Where's everyone?*
There's no one here. Where have the people gone?"

Em frowns. Her heart beats fasts and gives a skip.
"Josh, how long were we on that Ghost Train trip?"

A church clock chimes. *"It's midnight, Em! It's late!"*
In panic they dash through the Funfair's gate,

and as they race they hear a distant howl.
Josh shouts, *"The werewolf, Em. It's on the prowl!"*

Em gasps, *"We're almost back on our estate.*
Run, Josh, and don't look back! It's really late!

(Double trouble!)

THE NEXT DAY

The Ghost Train ride at Fangster's Fair
    turned out a scary date.
The two friends are in trouble —*deep* —
    for staying out so late.

Josh and Emma are both grounded,
    and *how* their parents moan.
The two pals have to keep in touch
    by text . . . and mobile phone.

The Ghost Train's weirdo journey
    and its shocks are left behind,
but even now that werewolf's howl
    still echoes in the mind,
        still
            echoes
                in
                    the
                        mind . . .

                        (The end . . .
                        or is it . . . ?)